# ZATHURA
## A SPACE ADVENTURE

"Mom!" Danny Budwing yelled. "Mom!"

Walter and Danny's mother stopped at her sons' bedroom door.

"Walter!" she said. "Get off your brother. Honestly, if you don't stop pulling on his nose like that, it'll end up looking like an elephant's trunk."

"Oh yeah?" said Walter. "Then he'll need the ears to match." He let go of Danny's nose and grabbed his ears.

"Enough!" Mrs. Budwing shouted.

"Danny started it. Look what he did," Walter yelled, picking up his walkie-talkie. The antenna was dangling by a wire. "See? He breaks everything."

"I'm sure he didn't mean to," Mrs. Budwing said.

"Was an accident," Danny mumbled.

From downstairs, Mr. Budwing called to his wife, "We're going to be late!"

Mrs. Budwing gave her sons a kiss good-bye. "I set some dinner out in the kitchen. Dad and I shouldn't be too late."

"Can't you take him with you?" Walter whined.

# ZATHURA
## A SPACE ADVENTURE

WRITTEN AND ILLUSTRATED BY
# CHRIS VAN ALLSBURG

HOUGHTON MIFFLIN COMPANY
BOSTON 2002

*To Anna, My Little Space Ranger*

Copyright © 2002 by Chris Van Allsburg

www.houghtonmifflinbooks.com

*Library of Congress Cataloging-in-Publication Data*

Van Allsburg, Chris.
Zathura : a space adventure / Chris Van Allsburg.
p. cm.
Summary: Left on their own for an evening, two boisterous brothers
find more excitement than they bargained for in a mysterious and
mystical space adventure board game.
ISBN 0-618-25396-3 (hardcover)
[1. Play. 2. Games.]  I. Title.
PZ7.V266 Zat 2002
[Fic]—dc21
2002001751

Manufactured in the United States of America
LBM 10 9 8 7 6 5 4 3 2 1

After their parents left, Walter sat down in front of the television.

"Can me and you go out and play catch together?" Danny asked.

"It's 'you and I,'" said Walter, "not 'me and you,' and the answer is no."

But Danny really wanted to play. He threw Walter his hat, but Walter just ignored him. Then he tossed him a baseball, and beaned him on the head.

Walter jumped up. "All right, you little fungus, now you're really going to get it." Danny bolted out of the room, down the hall, and out the front door, with Walter close behind. They ran into the park across the street, but Danny couldn't outrun his brother. Walter tackled him.

"I'm telling!" Danny squealed, as Walter got a grip on his nose and pulled. Then he let go.

"Hey, what's that?" he said. Right next to the boys was a long thin box resting against a tree. Walter got off his brother and picked it up.

"Aw, it's just some dumb old game. Here," he said, poking Danny in the stomach with the box, "it's for babies like you." He trotted off as Danny read the words on the box, JUMANJI, A JUNGLE ADVENTURE. Danny stuck the game under his arm and ran home after his brother.

Back inside, Danny looked at the box. It was covered with pictures of jungle animals. He took out dice, some tokens, and a very plain game board. Walter was right, it was a babyish game and probably boring, too. Danny started to put it away but discovered, jammed tightly into the bottom of the box, another board. He banged the box on the floor, and out it popped.

This board was more interesting. It showed flying saucers, rockets, and planets in outer space, with a path of colored squares leading from Earth to a purple planet called Zathura and back to Earth.

Danny put a token on Earth, then rolled the dice. After he'd moved along the path, something surprising happened. A buzzing sound came from the board and, with a click, a small green card popped out of the edge right in front of him. He picked it up and read, "'Meteor showers, take evasive action.'"

"Hey Walter," Danny started to say, "what does eva—" when he was interrupted by a noisy *rat-a-tat-tat* sound coming from the roof.

Walter looked up from the television. "Holy smoke," he said, "must be a hail storm!" "It's not hail!" shouted Danny, holding up the card. "It's meteors."

The noise grew louder, like a thousand golf balls bouncing off the roof. The room got so dark, Walter turned on the lights. Then—KABOOM—a rock the size of a refrigerator fell through the ceiling and crushed the television.

"See," Danny said, "I told you. Meteors."

Walter stared at the hole in the ceiling. "Okay," he agreed, "meteors. But how'd it get so dark so fast?" Through the hole he could see what was left of his parents' bedroom, and beyond that, a black, star-filled sky. "It looks like night up there."

"It's not night," said Danny. "It's outer space."

"What are you talking about? Jeez, outer space," Walter muttered as he went to the front door. "We just lost track of time. It's night, that's all." He threw open the door and almost took a step outside before he realized there was no outside there anymore. At least, not the one he expected.

"See," said Danny, "outer space." He led Walter back to the living room and showed him the Zathura game board and the card. Walter sat with his head in his hands, gazing at the path of colored squares that wound around the board and ended back at Earth.

"Looks like," said Danny, "we keep on playing or we're up here forever."

"Great," said Walter. "Up here, with you, forever." He took a deep breath, put a token on Earth, then rolled the dice and moved along the path. The board started buzzing, and—*click*—a card popped out. He studied it silently, then tossed the card on the board.

Danny leaned forward and read: "'The polarity on your gravity belt is reversed.' I wonder what that means?" He looked up, but Walter was gone.

"Walter!" he called out.

"Up here," answered Walter. Danny looked up and saw his brother pressed against the ceiling. "I've lost my gravity."

"That's not all you're going to lose," Danny said nervously, because he could see that Walter was being pulled slowly toward the hole in the ceiling— and a lonely trip into outer space.

Walter realized it too and started clawing at the ceiling, but he couldn't keep himself from moving closer and closer to the hole.

Danny looked around. Lying next to the meteor was the cord from the shattered television. He tossed it to Walter, who knotted it tightly to his belt. Danny grabbed the end of the cord and tied his brother to the sofa.

Danny rolled the dice and moved his token along the path. *Click.* Out popped another card: "'Your gyroscope is malfunctioning.'" Suddenly the house tilted. Everything in the room slid to one side, and Danny got buried under a mountain of furniture. He slowly dug himself out, clutching the game, only to find that Walter was floating back toward the hole in the ceiling.

Danny tied him to the sofa again and handed up the dice. Walter rolled and got his gravity back, dropping to the floor with a thud. Danny moved his piece and handed him his card. "'Your robot is defective,'" Walter read.

From the hallway came the sound of rattling metal and a steady *clank, clank, clank.* The boys stared at the doorway as a shiny silver robot stepped into view. He was having trouble walking on the tilted floor. His head rotated back and forth and seemed to freeze on Walter. The robot's eyes lit up and he spoke in an odd mechanical voice: "Emergency, emergency, alien life form. Must destroy." His clawlike metal hands snapped open and shut.

"Uh-oh," Danny whispered, "I think he's talking about you." Fortunately, when the robot stepped forward he missed the door, banged into the wall, and fell to the floor. He got up and did it again. And then again.

"Better hurry up and roll," said Walter, "before he makes it in here."

Danny rolled the dice and took his card: "'You pass too close to Tsouris 3, gravity greatly increased.'"

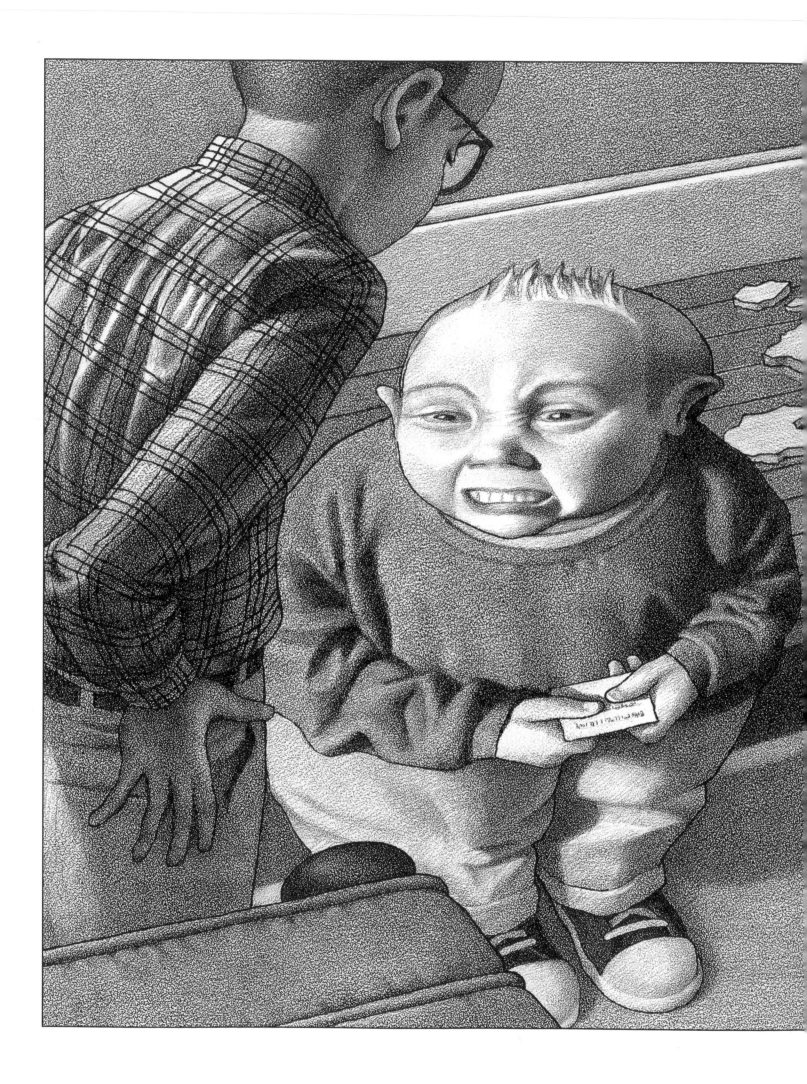

The room began to level out, but something strange was happening to Danny. Walter looked at him. "Holy smoke," he said. Danny was getting shorter, and wider too. Soon he was about the shape and size of a large beach ball.

"Waaalter," he said in a low voice. "I feeeel verrrry heeeavy."

"Destroy alien life forms," the robot repeated from the hall as he picked himself up again. This time he made it through the door and headed for Walter.

Danny yelled to his brother, "Puuush meee!"

"What?" said Walter.

"Puuush meee," Danny yelled again. "Juuust puuush meee."

Walter bent down and gave his brother a shove. Danny rolled across the room and, like a giant bowling ball, knocked the robot over and flattened his legs. "Did I geeet hiiim?" asked Danny, who couldn't see because he'd rolled up against a wall and was upside down.

Walter pushed him back to the game board. "You sure did," he said, patting his brother's head. "You were terrific."

Walter picked up the dice and rolled. He took his card, and his hand trembled as he read, "'Zorgon pirate ship launches photon attack.'"

Through the window, the boys saw a spaceship. Two points of light shot from the ship and headed directly for the Budwing house. The first one hit the chimney and sent bricks falling into the fireplace. The second hit the upstairs bathroom. Water began dripping down from the hole in the ceiling.

Walter handed the dice to Danny, who had a hard time lifting his short, heavy arm. He rolled, and as Walter moved his token for him, he slowly returned to his normal shape. A card popped out. Danny read it silently. "This is bad," he said. "'Zorgon pirate boards your vessel.'"

The room shook as the spaceship banged up against the house. The boys heard footsteps on the roof. Through the opening in the ceiling they saw someone or something climb through the hole in the roof and enter the room above them. Danny and Walter moved to the hallway, standing behind the flattened robot. They held each other, too terrified to move. A humming sound came from their feet. They looked down and saw the robot's eyes light up.

He lifted his head, fixed his eyes on the hole in the ceiling, and spoke: "Alien life form, must destroy." His clawlike hands twitched but he couldn't get up.

Danny and Walter helped him to his feet. He staggered forward as the pirate's scaly tail and lizardlike legs swung down from the hole. The robot lifted one of his claws and snapped it sharply around the creature's tail.

The Zorgon howled, jerking himself back through the hole, with the robot still attached. He thrashed and wailed, banging against the walls overhead. Then, minus one arm, the robot dropped down through the hole. The boys heard the Zorgon scramble across the roof and saw the flash of his rockets as his ship sped away.

It seemed hopeless. The robot's eyes were dark again. They'd been playing almost three hours, and their tokens rested a galaxy away from Zathura and twice that far from Earth. "We're never going to make it," said Walter.

"Sure we are," answered Danny. He handed the dice to his brother. "Me and you, together. We can do it."

Walter cradled the dice in his hand and sighed. "'You and I,'" he said wearily. "'You and I.'" He looked at his little brother, who was grinning.

"That's right," said Danny. "Together."

Walter rolled the dice, a one and a two. He moved his token to the only black square on the board. The card popped out. "'You have entered a black hole,'" Walter read. "'Go back in time, one hour for each mark on the dice.'"

He jumped up and looked around the room. "You see any black holes?"

His brother pointed to the floor. A black spot was slowly spreading under Walter's feet, like a perfectly round puddle of ink. At first Walter thought he was sinking into it, but it was the hole that was rising. He tried to run but could not feel his feet. Then, as the hole rose higher, he couldn't feel his legs, either. "What's going on?" he cried.

Danny looked below the disklike hole. "Walter," he said, "the bottom part of you is gone." As the hole rose higher and higher, there was less and less of Walter, until only his head remained. Danny tried to pull on the hole to save what was left of his brother, but his hands passed through the blackness as if it were made of smoke. His chin dropped to his chest and he began to sob.

"Danny," Walter called softly. Danny looked up at his brother's floating head. "Danny," he began, "I never told you this, but I . . ." And that was all he got to say, because the hole kept rising, past his mouth, his nose, and finally right over the top of his head.

Walter was completely swallowed up, floating in empty darkness. He closed his eyes as he began to spin, plunging head over heels through pitch-black space. Then, *thud*, he landed hard on his knees. There was something in his arms, something wriggling around.

He opened his eyes and found himself back in the park by his house. He had an arm wrapped tightly around Danny's neck and a hand gripping the boy's nose. "I'm telling," Danny squealed.

Walter let go and fell back on the grass. He was dizzy, very dizzy. Danny jumped up and started to run, but stopped. "Hey," he said, "what's that?" He went to a tree and picked up a box resting against the trunk. He held the box out to Walter. "Look," he said, "it's some kind of game."

Walter grabbed it. "Hey, give it back," said Danny.

His big brother got to his feet. "You don't want to play this," he said. "Trust me, I tried it once." He went over to a trash can and jammed the box deep inside. "Come on," he said, "I've got a better idea. Let's go play catch."

Danny smiled. "You mean together, me and you?"

Walter put his arm around his brother. "Yeah, that's right," he said. "Me and you, together."

FIC          Van Allsburg, Chris.
VAN
             Zathura.

$18.00                        YPVE59644

| DATE | | | |
|---|---|---|---|
|  |  |  |  |
|  |  |  |  |
|  |  |  |  |
|  |  |  |  |
|  |  |  |  |
|  |  |  |  |
|  |  |  |  |
|  |  |  |  |
|  |  |  |  |
|  |  |  |  |
|  |  |  |  |
|  |  |  |  |